TABLE OF CONTENTS

CHAPTER ONE

A new puzzle

One afternoon, Baba brought out a new puzzle.

"Want to join me, Yasmin?" he asked.

Yasmin looked at the box. It had a picture of a village. The box read "1000 Pieces"!

"That's a lot of pieces,"

Yasmin said.

Baba hugged her. "Don't

worry. We'll work on it together."

They set up their work space

on the coffee table. "We'll make

the edges first," Baba said. "And

then we'll fill in the middle."

Yasmin and Baba looked
through all 1,000 pieces to find
the edges. Every time she spotted
a piece with a straight side,
Yasmin exclaimed, "Found one!"

As they worked, they sorted the other pieces by colour. They kept at it until dinner time.

Later that evening, Yasmin came to say goodnight to Baba. He was still working on the puzzle! His back was bent. His eyes were squinted.

"Aren't you tired, Baba?"

Yasmin asked, yawning.

Baba didn't even look up.

"Just a few more pieces, jaan,"

he murmured. "Night, night."

CHAPTER TWO

Not feeling well

The next morning, Baba was lying in bed. Yasmin came to find out why he wasn't at breakfast.

"I feel all achy," Baba said.

"Let me fix you, Baba," Yasmin said. She went to get her doctor's bag.

Yasmin took his temperature. She made him open his mouth and say, "Aah". She even checked his pulse.

"How do you know all this, jaan?" Baba asked.

Yasmin smiled. "Ali's dad spoke at our school last week," she explained. "His name is Dr Tahir. He works at the hospital."

"What did Dr Tahir say?"
Baba asked.

"He always asks his patients
lots of questions," Yasmin said.
She took a notepad and pen
from her kit.

"Tell me your symptoms,
please," she said.

Baba groaned. "My back hurts," he said. "And my eyes."

Yasmin wrote that down.

"Runny nose or cough?" she asked.

Baba shook his head no.

"Did you fall down?" she guessed. "Maybe that's why your back hurts."

Baba shook his head again.

"Too much screen time?" Yasmin asked. "That might hurt your eyes."

Just then, Mama came in with some hot chai.

"Let your baba rest, Yasmin," she said.

CHAPTER THREE

Doctor's orders

Yasmin read over her notes in the living room.

She had followed all the advice from Dr Tahir. But she still didn't know what was wrong with Baba.

Being a doctor was hard.

Yasmin thought she might
cheer up Baba by getting more
work done on their puzzle. She
leaned over and began looking
for pieces.

Yasmin hunched her

shoulders as she leaned. She

squinted her eyes as she tried to

find the right pieces. She worked

for a long time.

When she finally stood up,
her back twinged. "OW!" she
said. Then she said, "Aha!"

Yasmin ran to her parents'
room.

"Baba! Your back is hurting because you worked on the puzzle for too long!" Yasmin said. "And your eyes too!"

Baba laughed and rubbed his back. "I think you're right, jaan! So, how can I get better?" he asked.

"Rest," Yasmin replied. "And no more than an hour a day on puzzles."

Baba gave Yasmin a hug.

"That's good advice, Dr Yasmin!"

Think about it, talk about it

* Yasmin gives Baba advice that helps him. Have you ever given advice to your family or relatives? Did it help them?

* Yasmin does the puzzle with Baba and by herself. What are some activities you like doing with your family? What are some activities you like doing by yourself? How is it different doing an activity alone and with someone?

* Do you think Yasmin might want to be a doctor when she grows up? What do you want to do when you grow up? Make a list of five things you might want to try.

Learn Urdu with Yasmin!

Yasmin's family speaks both English and Urdu. Urdu is a language from Pakistan. Maybe you already know some Urdu words!

baba father

chai tea with milk and spices

hijab scarf covering the hair

jaan life; a sweet nickname for a loved one

kameez long tunic or shirt

kitaab book

nana grandfather on mother's side

nani grandmother on mother's side

salaam hello

shukriya thank you

Pakistan fun facts

Yasmin and her family are proud of their Pakistani culture. Yasmin loves to share facts about Pakistan!

Pakistan is on the continent of Asia, with India on one side and Afghanistan on the other.

The word Pakistan means "land of the pure" in Urdu and Persian.

Many languages are spoken in Pakistan, including Urdu, English, Saraiki, Punjabi, Pashto, Sindhi and Balochi.

Malala Yousafzai and Abdus Salam are two people who won the Nobel Prize from Pakistan.

Pakistan's Edhi Foundation operates the world's largest ambulance network.

Pakistan has the largest canal-based irrigation system in the world.

Listen to your heart!

SUPPLIES:

- scissors
- 2 small balloons
- 2 small funnels
- tape or rubber bands
- about 60 cm of clear plastic tubing

STEPS:

1. Snip the ends off of the balloons.

2. Pull a balloon over the big end of each funnel.

3. Make sure the balloon is pulled tight and flat against each funnel. Wrap with tape or a rubber band to secure the funnels.

4. Place one end of the tubing into each funnel stem. If the tubing doesn't fit snugly, tape the tubing to the funnels.

5. Make sure the room is quiet and place one balloon end over your heart. Put the other end to your ear to hear your heartbeat!

Saadia Faruqi is a Pakistani American writer, interfaith activist and cultural sensitivity trainer featured in *O, The Oprah Magazine*. She also writes books for children, such as *Yusuf Azeem Is Not A Hero*, and other books for children. Saadia is editor-in-chief of *Blue Minaret*, an online magazine of poetry, short stories and art. Besides writing books, she also loves reading, binge-watching her favourite shows and taking naps. She lives in Houston, Texas, USA, with her family.

Hatem Aly is an Egyptian-born illustrator whose work has been featured in multiple publications worldwide. He currently lives in beautiful New Brunswick, Canada, with his wife, son and more pets than people. When he is not dipping cookies in a cup of tea or staring at blank pieces of paper, he is usually drawing books. One of the books he illustrated is *The Inquisitor's Tale* by Adam Gidwitz, which won a Newbery Honor and other awards, despite Hatem's drawings of a farting dragon, a two-headed cat and stinky cheese.

Join Yasmin on all her adventures!

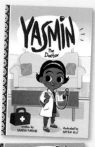

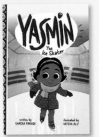

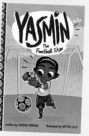

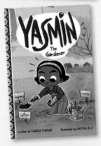

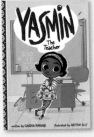

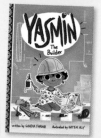